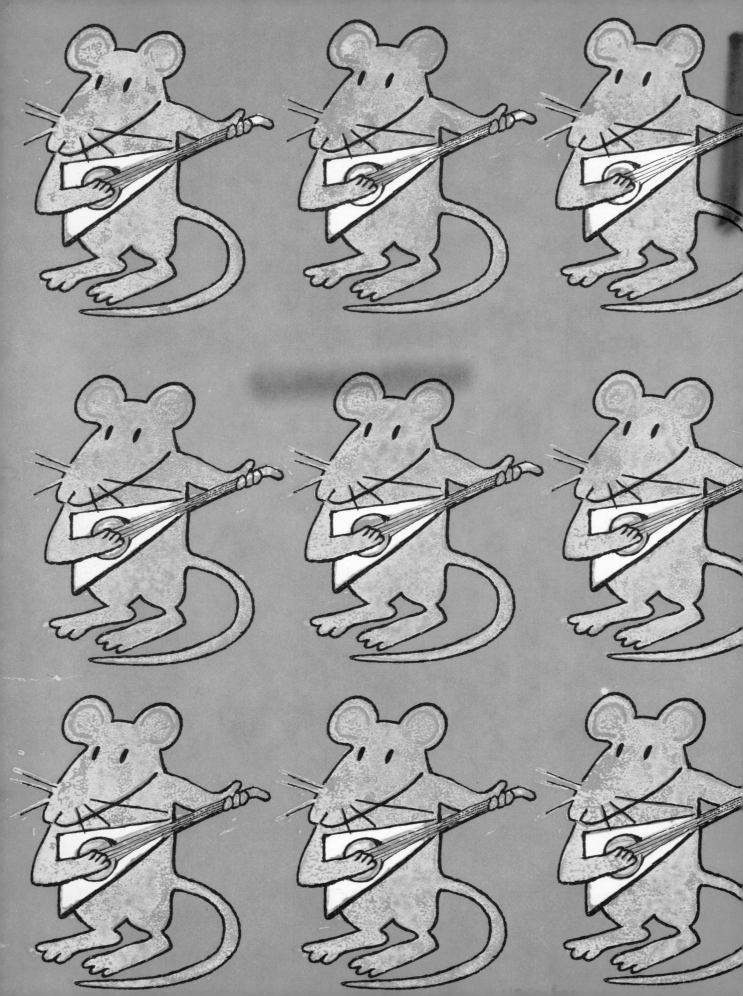

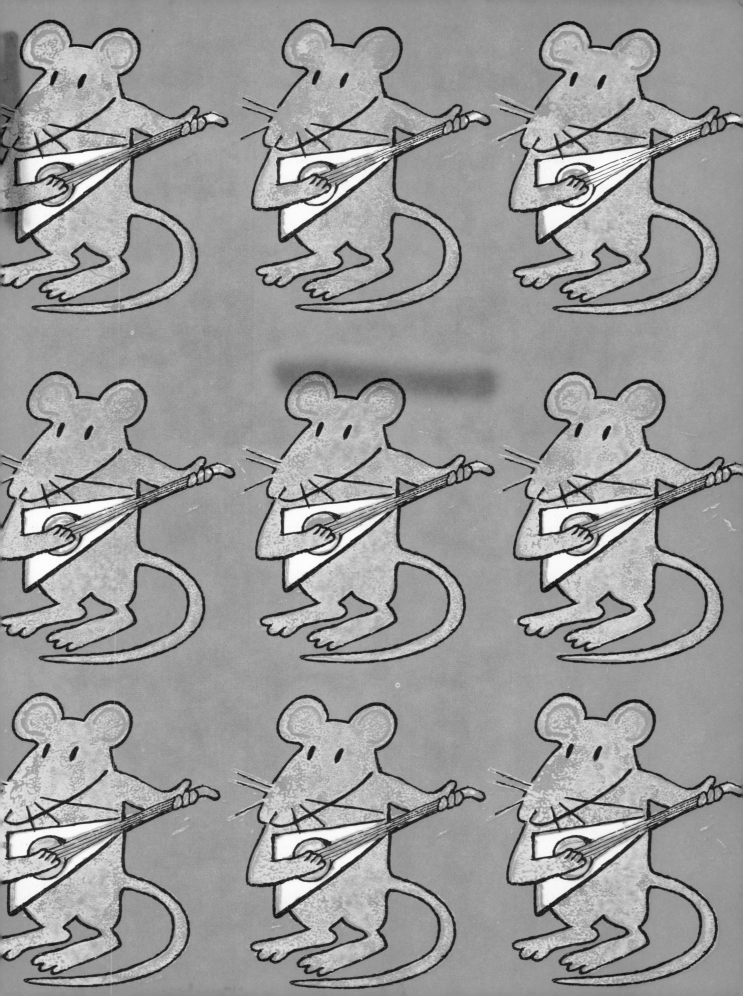

TRUBLOFF

The Mouse who wanted to play the Balalaika

written and illustrated
by
John Burningham

Random House
New York

First Random House Edition 1965

© Copyright, 1964, by John Burningham

All rights reserved under International and Pan-American Copyright
Conventions. Published in New York by Random House, Inc., and
in London, England, by Jonathan Cape Limited

Library of Congress Catalog Card Number: 65-18166

Manufactured in the United States of America

TRUBLOFF

**The Mouse
who wanted to play
the Balalaika**

This is a picture of the Trub family,
and here is a story about one of the
mice, whose name was Trubloff.

Trubloff was born at an inn. The inn was part of a little village in Central Europe, where the winters were very cold and snowy.

He lived with his father, mother, sisters and brothers in a house which they had made behind the panelling of the Parlour Bar.

On most nights there were musicians in the Parlour Bar — gypsies who wandered from village to village, playing at the inns. In return they received food, drink, and sometimes money.

Trubloff used to sit and listen to them playing, often until it was long past his bedtime.

Then his mother would have to come and look for him. "You're a naughty mouse, Trubloff. You're never in bed when the others are," she would tell him. "But I love to hear the music, and watch the gypsies play," he would say. He was nearly always the last young mouse in bed and was often scolded by his parents, but when his mother came for him, he had to go.

One evening, Trubloff went to see old Nabakoff, the craftsman mouse, who asked him why he was always listening to the music. "Because I love it," said Trubloff. "Well," said Nabakoff, "I'd better make you a balalaika." Trubloff was overjoyed.

Old Nabakoff told him that he would have to wait for two or three days. Impatiently Trubloff paced up and down, day and night.

Now the innkeeper had been kept awake by the noise that the Trubs made with their scuffling and chattering. (Trubloff was one of the noisiest.) He had tried to make his old cat go after them, but the cat was not really interested, because he got plenty of food from the customers in the Bar.

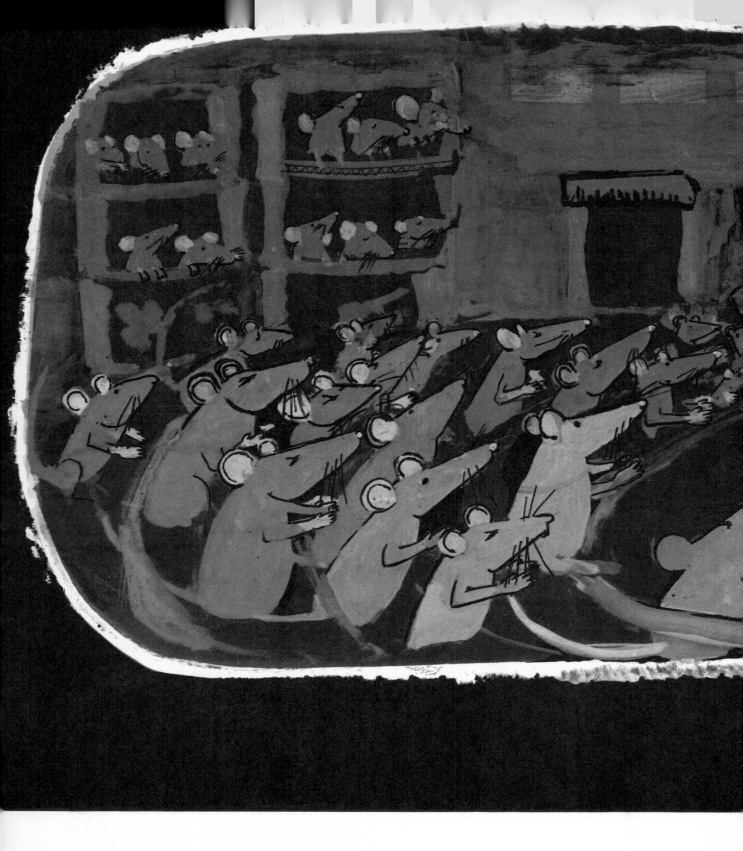

When Trubloff finally went to bed, he dreamed that he was the greatest balalaika-player in the whole country. In his dream, the

conductor of the orchestra stood humbly back while the audience clapped and clapped. They could not have enough of his playing.

Nabakoff finished the balalaika and gave it to Trubloff, who rushed off to a corner where he could not be heard. But he found that playing the balalaika was not easy.

In the Bar one evening, an old gypsy, who was himself playing the balalaika, heard the strange noises coming from Trubloff's instrument. He looked down and saw Trubloff. "Hello, mouse," he said. "So you want to be a musician, do you?" Trubloff replied that he did. "Let's have a look at you," said the gypsy. Trubloff nervously went over, carrying his balalaika. "It's a pity," said the old man. "I could have given you lessons, but we are leaving tonight." Trubloff was very disappointed.

But then he had an idea: he would hide in one of the gypsies' sleighs and travel with them.

He did not dare to tell his parents. He knew that they would never agree.

He took his warm coat, some food, and, of course, his balalaika, and when he thought nobody was looking, he found a good hiding-place in one of the sleighs.

The gypsies said goodbye to the innkeeper, and then they were off, travelling into the night.

As soon as they were some distance from the village, Trubloff cautiously came out from the old gypsy's pocket into which he had climbed as the sleigh sped over the snow.

The old man was very surprised to see him, but when Trubloff reminded him about the lessons, he remembered, and said that he would teach him to play.

The gypsies travelled from inn to inn, playing and dancing. Trubloff always listened to the music and the old gypsy gave him lessons. He was learning quite fast, and the old man was pleased with his little pupil.

Now the Trub family had looked in vain for Trubloff, and Mrs. Trub became ill with the strain of it all. But then an old water rat told them that he had been seen leaving with the gypsies, and one of Trubloff's sisters bravely volunteered to go out and make a search.

Meanwhile the gypsies travelled on.

One night, while the gypsies were sheltering in a barn, Trubloff's sister arrived on skis. All the gypsies were asleep except for the old man, who was giving Trubloff a lesson. Trubloff was startled to see his sister. "You must come home at once," she said. "Our mother is very ill."

She had brought with her an extra pair of skis for Trubloff so that they would be able to travel home much faster.

The two mice said goodbye to the old gypsy, and set off towards home on their skis.

At night they stayed wherever they could find the best shelter. Sometimes they had to curl up in the snow and sleep as best they could, but on other nights they were able to build a little fire.

Then came a terrible day when they were caught in a blizzard. This frightened them so much that they wondered whether they would ever get home to see their mother.

But the next day the sky was clear, and they felt sure that, over the next hill, they would find their own village.

At last they arrived and rushed up
to their mother's room. Both parents
were so overjoyed to see Trubloff

home, safe and sound, that they were not as severe in their scolding as they would otherwise have been. But Trubloff had to promise that he would not run off again without telling them.

Now in spite of their joy at Trubloff's return, Mr. and Mrs. Trub were still very worried. They had heard that the innkeeper was going to bring in some fierce farm cats to drive them and their children out of the inn. Mr. and Mrs. Trub did not know where they would go.

But on that very same evening, the innkeeper was in difficulties. The musicians who were to have played at the inn had not arrived, and the customers in the Parlour Bar were becoming impatient.

Trubloff had an idea. He went as close as he dared to the innkeeper and asked if he might be the musician for that evening. The innkeeper was amazed to see a mouse with a balalaika, but he had to admit, after hearing him, that Trubloff played well.

The innkeeper was so pleased with Trubloff that he told the Trubs they could stay on at the inn for as long as they wanted.

Mrs. Trub soon recovered from her illness now that her worries were over.

Trubloff's brothers and sisters learned to play instruments too. They formed a little band and often played in the Bar. Customers travelled great distances just to come and hear his music, and Trubloff's band became famous.

Now nobody knows exactly where to find the little inn which has a mouse band playing in the Parlour Bar.

But if you were to see a mouse on skis, it might well be Trubloff, and if you were to follow him, you might find the inn.

THE END

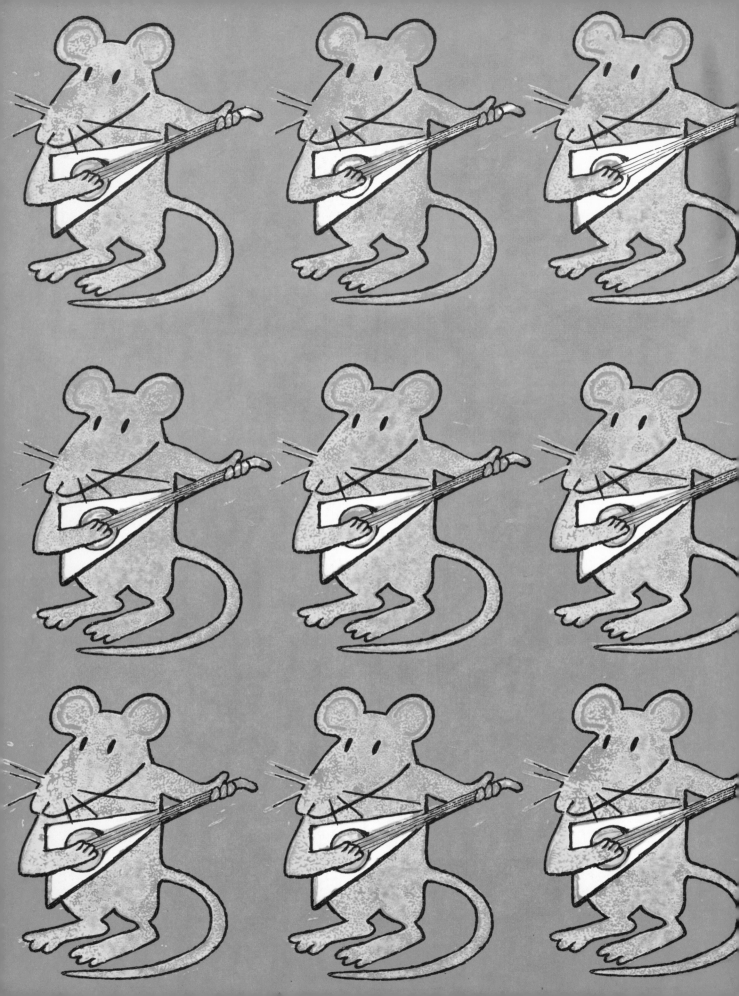